nickelodeon The

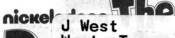

PICK YOUR PATH:
BANANAPALOOZA!

GROSSET & DUNLAP
Published by the Penguin Group
Penguin Group (USA) Inc., 375 Hudson Street, New York, New York 10014, USA
Penguin Group (Canada), 90 Eglinton Avenue East, Suite 700, Toronto,
Ontario M4P 2Y3, Canada (a division of Pearson Penguin Canada Inc.)
Penguin Books Ltd., 80 Strand, London WC2R 0RL, England
Penguin Group Ireland, 25 St. Stephen's Green,
Dublin 2, Ireland (a division of Penguin Books Ltd.)
Penguin Group (Australia), 250 Camberwell Road, Camberwell,
Victoria 3124, Australia (a division of Pearson Australia Group Pty. Ltd.)
Penguin Books India Pvt. Ltd., 11 Community Centre,
Panchsheel Park, New Delhi—110 017, India
Penguin Group (NZ), 67 Apollo Drive, Rosedale,
North Shore 0632, New Zealand
(a division of Pearson New Zealand Ltd.)
Penguin Books (South Africa) (Pty.) Ltd., 24 Sturdee Avenue,
Rosebank, Johannesburg 2196, South Africa

Penguin Books Ltd., Registered Offices: 80 Strand, London WC2R 0RL, England

ISBN 978-0-448-45571-6   10 9 8 7 6 5 4 3 2 1

nickelodeon **The PENGUINS of MADAGASCAR** ™

DREAMWORKS®

PICK YOUR PATH:
BANANAPALOOZA!

by Tracey West

Grosset & Dunlap
An Imprint of Penguin Group (USA) Inc.

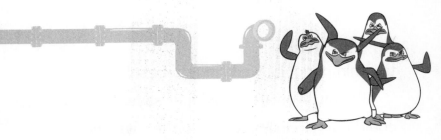

"Welcome to your new home," says Alice the zookeeper. She unlocks the door of your travel crate. "Try not to mess up the place while you're here."

You waddle out of your crate and into the penguin habitat at the New York Zoo. Four penguins are lined up in front of you.

"Hi," you begin after Alice leaves. "My name is—*ow!*"

One of the Penguins is pulling on your beak.

"Your clever disguise can't fool me," he says. "I know you're a spy!"

You push him off of you. "I'm not a spy! I'm an exchange penguin from the Southern California Zoo."

"His paperwork checks out, Skipper," says a

tall, thin penguin, waddling up beside you.

"I know, Kowalski," Skipper says. "But someone could have kidnapped him on the way here."

You're not sure what to make of all this. What kind of penguins are worried about spies?

"I'm from California. Honest," you say.

Skipper sticks his face up close to yours. "I'll be watching you, rookie. Any funny business and you'll be back in that crate before you can say double agent! Got it?"

You nod quickly. Skipper seems satisfied. "All right then. Private, give me your report on tonight's event."

"Tonight is the big Night at the Zoo event, sir," says Private, a short penguin with a friendly face. "After the zoo closes, the human zoo members will be sleeping over in tents. I overheard Alice say she expects five hundred people."

"Five hundred? That's a disaster waiting to

happen!" Skipper exclaims. He starts to pace back and forth. "We'll have to keep all the animals on lockdown. If the humans ever found out what happens between these walls in the dead of night, there would be big trouble."

"Greetings, Penguins!"

You turn to see that a skinny lemur wearing a crown made of leaves has bounded in. He's followed by a chubby aye-aye and a cute, short mouse lemur.

The skinny lemur stops when he sees you. "I must be seeing double. Maurice, did you put too much mango in my morning smoothie?"

"I'm a visiting penguin," you explain. "From California."

"Ah, the land of the sun and the fun and the parties on the beach!" he says. "I, King Julien, am very impressed."

He motions to the chubby aye-aye. "Maurice,

please be giving them the invitations."

"What is this?" Skipper asks suspiciously as Maurice hands him a piece of paper.

"It is an invite to my most marvelous party this evening!" King Julien says, opening his arms wide. "Bananapalooza!"

Skipper waddles up to him. "Oh no," he says sternly. "You can't have a party tonight. It's the Night at the Zoo. The humans will be here."

"Maybe you could have the party tomorrow night," Private helpfully suggests.

"But it *must* be tonight," King Julien says. "Bananapalooza always takes place in the month of Festivus on the night when the moon is shaped like a banana. And that is tonight."

"Banana, schmanana," says Skipper. "I forbid you to have that party!"

"And you are not going to be telling me what to do!" the king shoots back angrily.

He turns to you. "You look like a fun-loving, party penguin to me. Would you like to be helping us to make Bananapalooza most fabulous?"

"You're barking up the wrong penguin, Julien," Skipper snaps. "This rookie is one of us. And we're launching Operation Banana Split— we're going to squash Bananapalooza!"

If you want to stick with Skipper and the Penguins, go to page 24.

If you decide to help King Julien with Bananapalooza, go to page 39.

CONTINUED
FROM PAGE 30.

You have a feeling that giving Mort such an important job is not a very good idea. It might be safer to do this without him.

"Um, Mort, King Julien told me he needs you to polish his whiskers," you say.

"Really? Oh goody!" he cries. The little mouse lemur scampers off.

That leaves you and the Gorillas. You tiptoe past the sleeping beasts as quietly as you can. Then you slowly push the crate to the back of the habitat. It's so heavy! You'll never get it back to the lemur habitat by yourself.

Puffing and panting, you push the crate onto one of the zoo pathways. Now you see Alice's golf carts. She's nowhere around. You know they go very fast, but you've never driven one.

Next to the golf cart is a big wagon—the

kind that you push. It says "Banana Wagon" on the side. How convenient is that?

If you use the golf cart,
go to page 26.

If you use the banana wagon,
go to page 49.

CONTINUED FROM PAGE 48.

"Pick the lock, Kowalski," Skipper instructs.

Kowalski holds out a flipper, and Rico coughs up a lockpick from somewhere inside his gullet. Kowalski inserts it in the lock and jiggles it. The door swings open and all of you slide into the room, skidding to a stop.

Just then, you hear a voice coming down the path.

"I saw something strange on the security cameras."

It's Alice talking into her radio!

If you all make a run for it, go to page 38.

If you all hide and hope Alice doesn't see you, go to page 53.

"If you kidnap King Julien, you stop the party," you reason. "I think I like Private's idea."

"My thoughts exactly!" says Skipper. He thoughtfully rubs his chin. "We'll need the element of surprise. Follow my lead, lads."

Minutes later you are holding a potted plant in front of you and tiptoeing down the path to the lemur habitat with the other Penguins. Skipper's idea seems to be working. Nobody notices you.

When you get to the habitat, you hear King Julien yelling at Maurice and Mort inside his colorful bouncy house.

"We will be needing bananas! Many, many bananas!"

"He's there for the taking, boys," Skipper

whispers. "But we need a plan. We can't just run in and grab him."

"What if we lure Julien out of the bounce house, Skipper?" Private asks.

"Good idea," says Skipper. "But my lovely lady lemur costume is at the cleaner's."

Rico coughs up a long pin from his gullet. He holds it up, pointing to the bounce house.

"Deflating the bounce house. I like it," says Skipper. "But it could be dangerous."

"Maybe we could sneak up from behind and grab him," you suggest.

If you sneak up behind King Julien,
go to page 31.

If Rico deflates the bounce house,
go to page 45.

CONTINUED FROM PAGE 37.

You decide to check out Marlene's talent. You find her playfully swimming in the otter habitat.

"Hi there," you say. "I'm visiting from the Southern California Zoo. I'm helping Maurice find a new talent act for Bananapalooza. Some squirrel told me to see you."

"Oh, that's Fred," she said. "Well, he happens to be right. Give me a minute."

Marlene climbs out of the water, ducks into her little cave, and comes out wearing a tutu and juggling three balls in the air. It's impressive.

"That's not all," she says. She puts down the balls, then drags out two poles with a line strung between them and stands them upright. She shimmies up one pole and walks the tightrope.

Then she jumps down, somersaulting in the air.

"Ta da!" she cries.

"You're fantastic!" you say. "Let's bring this act to Maurice."

Marlene does the act for King Julien and Maurice, and they love it, too.

"The banana moon will be rising soon," King Julien says. "We have very much left to do!"

The next two hours fly by in a whirlwind. You peel hundreds of bananas and help the cute, little lemur, Mort, string sparkling lights all over the zoo.

At seven o'clock, the zoo closes. The visitors pour through the gates with their tents and sleeping bags. On the other side of the zoo, the animals head to the lemur habitat wearing their party clothes.

You start to get nervous. What if the visitors see the animals?

Then, suddenly, the zoo is plunged into darkness! You realize that Skipper and his crew have stopped the party *and* the campout. But they also may have just saved the day!

THE END

CONTINUED FROM PAGE 25.

"I like Rico's idea," you say. "An explosion sounds cool."

"We'll need to find the perfect location," Skipper says. "Somewhere out of the way. When the zoo closes, we'll go scouting."

The next few hours pass by quickly. You swim and let the zoo visitors take your picture. When the zoo closes, Skipper leads a scouting mission.

You swiftly travel down the zoo pathways. The four commandos point out the different habitats, the Zoovenir Shop, and other highlights. As you pass the monkey house, you're surprised to see some skunks under a tree. There are no skunks at the Southern California Zoo!

"They are natural residents of the park," Kowalski explains. "They don't bother us, and we don't bother them."

Skipper leads you to the top of a hill behind the garages that hold the zoo's golf carts.

"It's perfect!" Skipper says happily. "Okay, Rico, show us what you've got."

To your surprise, Rico upchucks several large fireworks from deep within his gullet. It's weird, but you're impressed.

"Fireworks," you say. "*Hmm.* Humans like fireworks, don't they? They might not be afraid."

Skipper doesn't look happy that you're challenging his idea.

"Can you think of anything better, rookie?" he asks.

If you agree that fireworks are the way to go, go to page 42.

If you suggest another idea, go to page 59.

CONTINUED FROM PAGE 46.

"Maybe he went left," you say.

You speed around the corner, making a left turn—and run right into a troop of girl scouts!

"Freeze, boys!" Skipper commands.

You stop, not moving a muscle. One of the girl scouts spots you.

"Look at those penguin dolls!" she cries.

"They're so lifelike!" says another girl. She scoops you up. "You'll make a great souvenir."

You and the others are helpless as the girls carry you off. You know it won't be long before they figure out you're real. And that means you'll be in big trouble with Alice!

THE END

"Sure, I'll be your entertainment director!" you tell King Julien.

"Marvelous!" the lemur cries. "Maurice, please to be showing our new friend the ropes."

"Sure thing," says Maurice with an evil gleam in his eye. "Follow me, kid."

Maurice leads you through the zoo. He stops in front of a small crate.

"We'll have our meeting in here," he says.

"Uh, sure," you say. Suddenly—*BAM!*

Maurice slams the crate shut. "Bein' the king's main man is my job," he says. "Sorry, but you're going back to California."

You're relieved. These East Coast animals are way too kooky for you!

THE END

CONTINUED FROM PAGE 55.

Skipper makes the decision. "Let's fly, boys!"

You all charge toward the souvenir cart and grab onto a big bunch of helium balloons. The balloons lift you up, up into the sky. Kowalski is frantically trying to calculate wind speed and direction.

"Everyone lean to the right!" he yells.

You do, and this sends you soaring right above Maurice and the popcorn cart.

"Disengage!" Skipper cries.

Everyone lets go of the balloons and tumbles onto the popcorn cart below. The impact sends Maurice flying.

"Jump!" Skipper commands.

Skipper hits the ground first and grabs the cart handle before it can roll out of control.

The rest of you help him push the cart back to Penguin Headquarters.

Skipper is delighted. "Mission accomplished!" he says. He turns to you. "Rookie, keep an eye on Ringtail here while we go round up Maurice and Mort."

You salute. "Will do, sir!"

The other Penguins leave, and King Julien hops out of the popcorn cart.

"Oh, my dizzy head," he says. He shakes his fist at you. "I was wrong about you, California penguin. You are no fun at all. Now there can be no Bananapalooza!"

Suddenly, you hear a noise. You look up to see Maurice dropping down from the sky!

Go to page 28.

"I'm a penguin," you tell King Julien. "I guess I'll stick with these guys."

"Suit yourself, you party-pooping penguin," the king replies. "We don't want you coming to our party, anyway!"

The mammals storm off.

"All right, men," Skipper says. "We've got to stop Bananapalooza before the humans get here. Any ideas?"

Kowalski starts to scribble furiously on a pad. He holds up a complicated diagram. "If we disable the main generator, we can shut off all the power in the zoo. The humans would have to go home."

"Interesting," says Skipper.

"Or we could kidnap King Julien," says Private. "Then the humans could still have their sleepover."

"A good possibility," Skipper says. "What about you, Rico?"

The fourth, wild-eyed penguin grins. *"Boom!"*

Skipper seems to understand him perfectly. "Excellent idea. You create an explosion to frighten the humans away."

Then Skipper turns to you. "So what do you think, rookie?"

Your head is spinning. You thought you came here to eat fish and sit in the sun. Now you're in the middle of some kind of top secret mission.

If you like Private's idea the best,
go to page 13.

If you like Rico's idea the best,
go to page 18.

If you like Kowalski's idea the best,
go to page 47.

CONTINUED FROM PAGE 11.

You're not sure why, but there's something about the banana cart that seems suspicious to you. You decide to take the golf cart instead.

It's not easy pushing the crate onto the back of the golf cart, but you do it. Then you hop on the seat. You realize that you can't reach the pedals with your feet, so you jump to the floor. You'll just have to stick your head out the side and hope for the best.

You step on the gas, and the golf cart darts forward. You zip down the zoo pathway. Behind you, you hear Alice yelling, "My golf cart!"

You step on the gas harder and careen through the zoo. You make a right, then a left, then a right. Suddenly you see a sign for the lemur habitat and make the turn, your brakes squealing.

You crash into the habitat and the banana crate falls off, spilling bananas everywhere. King Julien is thrilled.

"So many beautiful bananas!" he cries, clapping his hands. "And now it is time to make a beautiful banana sculpture—of me! Penguin, please to be peeling and mashing all of these bananas."

That doesn't sound like much fun to you. King Julien is more demanding than you realized. You're starting to wonder if you should have stayed with Skipper and the Penguins.

If you sneak away to rejoin Skipper and the Penguins, go to page 34.

If you stick with King Julien, go to page 43.

**CONTINUED
FROM PAGE 23.**

"Just give me the king, kid," Maurice says. "You're not really one of those kooky Penguins, anyway."

That makes you think. Skipper has treated you like one of his men right from the start. You're a penguin, and penguins have to stick together.

"Sorry, Maurice," you say. "I *am* one of them."

You quickly grab the tub of popcorn butter and toss the butter on the ground. Maurice falls in the slippery goo just as Skipper and the others return.

"Nice work, rookie," Skipper tells you as Rico and Private tie up Maurice. "From now on, you're an honorary member of our squad!"

THE END

CONTINUED FROM PAGE 52.

You're feeling brave. "No problem. I'll get the bananas for you," you say.

"Most excellent!" King Julien cheers. "Mort, please accompany our brave new friend."

"Okeydoke," says the cute, little lemur in a high voice.

Mort leads you to the gorilla habitat. You hide behind a garbage can and scope out the situation. Two gorillas are snoozing in the sun. There's a huge crate of bananas behind them.

"That's Bada and Bing," Mort tells you. "They like to punch and hit!"

Suddenly you're not feeling so brave. "Those guys are pretty big," you say. "If they catch us, they'll hurt us."

"Mort will do anything for his beloved King

Julien!" the little lemur says.

You try to think. If you're quiet, you might be able to sneak past them and cart the bananas away. But if they wake up, you're done for.

You look at Mort. Maybe you could use him to create a distraction. With the Gorillas out of the way, it would be easy to grab the bananas.

If you sneak past the Gorillas,
go to page 10.

If you ask Mort to distract them,
go to page 61.

CONTINUED FROM PAGE 14.

"I like your spirit, rookie!" Skipper says. "Private, I want you and the rookie to commence Operation Kidnap."

"Will do, Skipper," Private says with a salute. He nods to you. "Follow me."

Private waddles out from behind his flowerpot and dashes to a nearby cleaning cart. He grabs a large garbage bag. Then the two of you press your bodies against the base of the bounce house. You slowly lift your head.

A bunch of palm fronds are sticking out of one of the open windows.

"It's Julien's crown!" you whisper to Private. "He's right there!"

He nods at you. You reach through the window and grab onto a pair of fuzzy shoulders.

You haul the lemur out through the window and stuff him into the bag Private is holding.

You and Private race back to the penguin habitat. He leads you underground to the Penguins' secret headquarters. Skipper is holding open the door to a large wall safe.

"In here, boys!" he tells you.

Private tosses the garbage bag in, and Skipper slams the door. You can hear muffled cries from inside the safe.

"And now we stand watch," Skipper says. "Tomorrow morning, when the visitors leave, we'll let him out."

The sun sets, and the visiting campers invade the zoo. Everything is quiet—until, suddenly, you hear disco music blaring outside. You rush out to see all of the zoo animals dancing and having fun! King Julien is singing on top of his throne.

"But if King Julien is out there . . ." A terrible

thought hits you: You kidnapped the wrong lemur by mistake!

You all rush back into Penguin Headquarters. Skipper throws open the door to the safe. Mort is there, wearing a party hat made of palm fronds.

"You found me!" he cries happily. "Is the game of hide-and-seek over now?"

"Sorry, Skipper," you say. "When I saw the hat, I thought he was King Julien."

"This is bad," Skipper says. "We couldn't stop Bananapalooza. There's only one thing to do."

"What's that, Skipper?" Private asks.

Skipper grabs Mort's party hat and puts it on his own head. "If we're all going down, we might as well join the party!"

THE END

"I'll get right on it," you tell King Julien.

Then you run away as fast as you can. You enter the penguin habitat. Skipper steps in front of you.

"Stop right there!" he commands. "No traitors allowed in here."

"I'm not a traitor," you tell him, thinking quickly. "I've been under cover."

Skipper's eyes widen. "Of course! Why else would a penguin run off with that ridiculous ringtail?" He motions to you. "Come with me, rookie."

Skipper leads you inside a fake cave that leads underneath the penguin habitat. You see that the Penguins have turned it into some kind of secret headquarters. Kowalski, Rico, and

Private are standing over a table studying plans. They look surprised to see you.

"It's okay—he went under cover," Skipper tells them. "All right, rookie, spill. What's King Julien up to?"

You tell him everything the king is planning. Skipper looks thoughtful. "It might be harder to stop this Bananapalooza than we thought."

"Maybe we could ask King Julien to move the party," Private suggests. "Somewhere the humans won't see it."

"That might work!" you say. "King Julien still thinks I'm on his side. I could try to convince him."

Skipper slaps you on the back. "Give it a try, rookie!"

You head back to the lemur habitat. King Julien hasn't even noticed you were gone. He's too busy describing how the sculpture should look.

"Make sure you capture the mystery in my

eyes," he says. "They're my best feature."

"Um, King Julien, I have an idea," you say. "In California, underground parties are the hottest thing. We could do it right—glow sticks, glittering lights, the whole thing."

"I don't like this idea at all," King Julien says, and your heart sinks. Then he throws up his arms. "I love it!"

Your great idea has saved the day. That night, the zoo animals gather underground for Bananapalooza. There's music, dancing, and a glow-in-the-dark sculpture of King Julien. The party is such a blast that even Skipper has fun!

THE END

Stealing bananas sounds dangerous.

"I'll help Maurice find some new talent," you say. You turn to Maurice. "What do you want me to do?"

"Ask around the zoo. See who's hot and who's not," Maurice replies.

"I can do that," you say confidently.

It's strange walking around the zoo. In California, you were always inside your habitat. But the animals here are very friendly. You wonder who you should talk to first.

If you talk to the otter,
go to page 15.

If you talk to the elephant,
go to page 56.

CONTINUED FROM PAGE 12.

You make a break for it, but Alice spots you.
"Hey! Penguins! Stop!" she yells.

"Split up!" Skipper yells. But you all head in the same direction, bumping into one another. You fall down like bowling pins. Alice grabs you.

"Must be a loose gate in your habitat," she says. "Guess I'll have to put you in lockup tonight."

"This is terrible," Skipper whispers. "Now there's nothing we can do to stop Bananapalooza! Looks like our secret agent operation is busted."

THE END

Who should you stick with? A penguin who thinks he's some kind of secret agent? Or a lemur who wants to have a party?

As long as you're just visiting, you might as well have some fun. You nod to King Julien.

"I'll help you with Bananapalooza," you say.

"Excellent!" the lemur says, clapping his hands. "Now let us all go make some plans."

You follow the Lemurs to their habitat, where Julien sits on his throne. The cute, short lemur waves a fan in front of the king's face.

King Julien unrolls a long scroll of paper.

"Here is our list of our most fabulous party ideas," he says. "We need a light-up dance floor, disco balls, confetti, and, of course, bananas prepared in the twenty-seven traditional ways . . ."

"I'll get right on it, Your Majesty," Maurice says.

"I was thinking that the party penguin here could be the entertainment director this year," King Julien says with a nod to you. "What do you say?"

Maurice looks upset. You wonder if you'll hurt his feelings if you take the job.

If you agree to become the entertainment director, go to page 21.

If you ask King Julien if you can do something else, go to page 51.

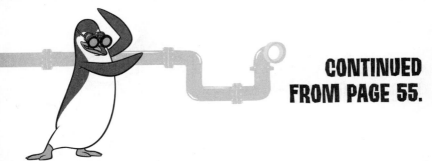

CONTINUED FROM PAGE 55.

"It may be difficult to control the trajectory of the balloons, sir," Kowalski points out.

"Good point," says Skipper. "Let's cut across Jumbo's habitat."

You follow the others into the elephant habitat. In your hurry to keep up with them, you knock into a barrel holding Jumbo's peanuts. The nuts spill all over the ground.

Suddenly you feel something grab you. It's Jumbo! He's got you in his trunk.

"You're not going anywhere until you clean that up!" Jumbo tells you.

"Y-y-y-yes, sir," you stammer nervously.

You just hope that your new friends will succeed in their mission without you.

THE END

CONTINUED FROM PAGE 19.

You don't want to upset Skipper. "Let's stick with the fireworks," you say.

Rico lights a match. With an excited gleam in his eye, he lights the fuses on the fireworks.

"Dive!" Skipper yells.

You all dive for cover as the fireworks shoot up into the sky. They explode in a dazzling display of colorful lights.

Just as you predicted, the humans aren't afraid. But that's okay. It distracts them from Bananapalooza. When you get back to your habitat, you find animals dancing to disco music. Maurice is juggling bananas. Mort is sculpting a statue of King Julien out of mashed fruit.

Skipper turns to the squad. "Boys, I command you to join in the fun!"

THE END

You're not sure if the Penguins will take you back.

"I'll get started right away," you say with a sigh.

You spend the next several hours peeling bananas, mashing bananas, and then trying to shape the sticky mess to look like King Julien. He bosses you around the whole time.

"No, no, no! My luscious eyelashes should be longer!"

"My ears are too pointy, you terrible penguin!"

"My nose is not kingly enough!"

Finally the sculpture satisfies the king. But your work isn't over. You still have to hang decorations, make punch, and string lights. By the time the banana-shaped moon rises in the sky, you're exhausted.

Even the Penguins can't stop King Julien. The party begins, and it's a wild night of dancing and fun. But the overnight visitors catch everything on their cameras. Soon images of the party at the zoo are all over the Internet.

The zoo hires extra security guards at night. The animals have to stay in their habitats. No more nighttime fun!

The worst thing is you have to live with the Penguins and they're all mad at you. Skipper calls you a traitor. You wish you had stuck with them from the start!

THE END

CONTINUED FROM PAGE 14.

"Nice idea, rookie, but I think we need to make a big move here," Skipper says. "Rico, pop that bounce house!"

Rico nods and darts out from behind his flowerpot. He climbs into the lemur habitat and runs up to the bouncy house. Then he stabs the pin into the puffed-up plastic.

Pop! The bouncy castle slowly begins to deflate. King Julien runs out screaming.

"The sky is falling! The sky is falling!" he yells. "Maurice, tell that misbehaving sky to stop right now!"

Maurice crawls out from under the deflated bouncy house and sees Rico holding the pin.

"Those Penguins did this," he says. "We've got to get you out of here, Your Majesty."

"After him, boys!" Skipper yells.

Maurice hoists King Julien over his shoulder. Then he jumps out of the lemur habitat, dumps King Julien into a popcorn cart, and they race off.

Skipper leads the way as you all chase after the popcorn cart. As Maurice pushes the cart into a crowd gathered in front of the gorilla habitat, you dart among the visitors' legs, trying to catch up. But when you pass through the crowd, you don't see Maurice—you've lost him.

If you make a left turn, go to page 20.

If you make a right turn, go to page 55.

"I like Kowalski's idea," you say.

"I agree," says Skipper. "A blackout is just what we need. We'll have to wait until the zoo closes."

You spend the rest of the day entertaining the visiting humans. After the zoo closes, Skipper puts the plan into action.

"Stealth mode, men," he orders.

The five of you climb out of the habitat and make your way toward the generator. The humans begin to enter the zoo, hauling sleeping bags with them. As you pass the lemur habitat, you hear King Julien barking orders at Maurice.

"No, no, no! We need more glitter on the banana piñatas!" he yells. "And nine disco balls is just not enough!"

You quickly reach the concrete powerhouse

in a secluded corner of the zoo.

"The control panel for the main generator is inside," Kowalski tells you. "But this building is kept locked for security reasons."

If Kowalski picks the lock on the powerhouse door, go to page 12.

If you and the others enter through a vent in the roof, go to page 57.

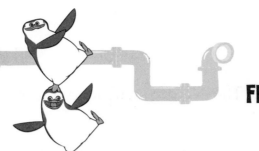

CONTINUED FROM PAGE 11.

You decide that using the golf cart is too risky. The banana wagon is just what you need. You make sure the coast is clear, then you run out and grab the wagon by the handles.

Suddenly, four penguins swoop down from the sky on a zip line. It's Skipper, Kowalski, Private, and Rico! They surround the banana wagon.

"What's going on?" you ask.

"Operation Banana Split!" Skipper tells you. "Cuff him, boys!"

Rico slaps a pair of cuffs on your flippers.

"Now let's load up these bananas," Skipper tells his crew.

You watch helplessly as the other Penguins load the crate onto the wagon. They take you back to the penguin habitat and lead you underground. They've got some kind of secret headquarters under there.

Rico and Private escort you to the brig, and Skipper slams the door shut.

"That banana wagon was the perfect trap," Skipper says proudly. "And you fell for it like a snowflake falling from the sky."

"Sorry, mate," Private says. "But you'll have to stay here until the visitors leave in the morning."

"And those bananas aren't going anywhere, either," Skipper promises.

You can't believe you fell for a trap! Even worse, there won't be any bananas for King Julien. You've failed.

THE END

You don't want to upset Maurice. "I'll take another job if you have one," you tell King Julien.

"Very well," says the lemur. "We will need bananas. Many, many bananas! I will need you to be stealing them from the gorilla house."

"Stealing?" you ask. "Can't we just ask the gorillas to donate them?"

"The gorillas and I are not speaking," King Julien says. "They're still angry that I beat them at the karaoke last year. Oh yes!"

Maurice steps between you. "Throwing this kid to the gorillas is kinda harsh, boss," he says. "Maybe the penguin could be my assistant. I need to dig up some new talent for the party, and that's going to take some work."

"But I am needing the bananas!" King Julien

says. He sighs. "I will leave it up to you, my new penguin friend. What would you like to do?"

If you steal the bananas,
go to page 29.

If you search for new talent,
go to page 37.

"Let's hide!" you say in a loud whisper.

The five of you scramble for cover under a table in the corner. Alice walks in and turns on the light. Luckily she doesn't see you.

"Must have been some squirrels," she mutters.

She leaves you alone in the powerhouse. Kowalski quickly goes to work on the control panel, frying the wires. Within seconds, the zoo plunges into darkness.

"Good work, Kowalski!" Skipper says.

In the distance, you hear the loud cries of disappointed visitors as Alice sends them packing for the night. When the coast is clear, you all make your way back to the penguin habitat.

On the way, you see the zoo animals gathered around the lemur habitat. Everyone looks disappointed. King Julien is wailing on his throne.

"No power! No disco balls! No music! This is most terrible!"

Maurice starts to shoo everyone away. "Sorry, folks. Bananapalooza is canceled."

Then he spots you and points. "This is all the fault of those party-pooping Penguins, everyone!"

The crowd of gorillas, elephants, monkeys, and other zoo animals turns to you and glares.

"It was for your own good!" Skipper tells them.

The animals look so unhappy. You wonder—did you make the right choice by sticking with the Penguins?

THE END

"Let's try going to the right," you say.

You zoom around the corner. Maurice is far ahead, pushing the popcorn cart to the top of a tall hill.

"We'll never catch up on foot. We need a shortcut," says Skipper. His eyes dart back and forth at his surroundings. Then he points.

"If we cut across the elephant habitat, it'll take us to the bottom of that hill," he says. Then he nods toward a souvenir stand selling helium balloons. "Or we could fly."

If you use the helium balloons to fly, go to page 22.

If you cut across the elephant habitat, go to page 41.

CONTINUED FROM PAGE 37.

You head to the elephant habitat to see Jumbo. He's taking a nap. You tap him on the trunk.

"Excuse me, but I'm looking for a new act for Bananapalooza," you begin.

Jumbo's eyes fly open. "Bananapalooza! You bet!" He jumps to his feet, and the ground shakes underneath you. "Check out my tap-dancing act!"

"Sure, let me just get out of the way," you say. But Jumbo is eager to impress you.

Stomp! Stomp! Stomp! He dances around the habitat. Before you can get away . . . *STOMP!* His foot misses you by an inch.

You wish you had never left California. This zoo is downright dangerous!

THE END

CONTINUED FROM PAGE 48.

"There's a vent in the roof," you say, pointing up. "An easy way in for penguins our size."

"Excellent thinking, rookie!" Skipper says.

You shimmy up a drainpipe to the roof, and the others follow. Then you enter through the vent and jump down onto the generator below. Kowalski quickly goes to work on the control panel, frying the wires. Within seconds, the zoo plunges into darkness.

As you make your way back to the penguin habitat, you see the disappointed visitors leaving the zoo. In the lemur habitat, King Julien looks defeated.

"No power, no party," he says sadly. "It looks like the Penguins are winning this one."

"Can you fix the generator?" you ask

Kowalski. "Now that the humans are gone, it couldn't hurt to have the party."

Kowalski shakes his head. "I don't have the parts to fix it. But perhaps my moonlight illuminator will work."

He rushes off to the penguin habitat and comes back wheeling a strange device made from a milk crate, an old umbrella, a mirror, and recycled glass bottles. He carefully aims the mirror at the banana-shaped moon and . . . *wham!*

Bright light floods the zoo. The animals cheer.

"Let Bananapalooza begin!" King Julien cries.

THE END

"I know something that really scares humans," you say. "Skunks! Their special smelly skills will get rid of those visitors for sure."

"Rookie, I like the way you think!" Skipper says. "Let's go talk to our stinky friends."

You and Skipper march back to the skunks.

"It's like this," Skipper begins. "In a little while this place is going to be crawling with humans. We need your help getting rid of them."

The skunks huddle together. Then one of them walks toward you.

"It's like dis," he says in a New York accent. "We'll do it. But we want fish bones. Every night for two weeks."

"It's a deal!" Skipper says. "Follow us to the campsite."

Soon you're all at the field behind the elephant habitat where the visitors are setting up tents and sleeping bags. Skipper nods to the skunks.

"You're on!"

The skunks march in single file onto the field. Then they start to sing:

"Shake, shake, shake! Shake, shake, shake! Shake your booty!"

The skunks wiggle their butts to the song. Then they turn around.

POOOOOOOOF! Smelly stuff shoots out. The campers run away screaming. Soon the park is empty.

Skipper is pleased. "Mission accomplished!"

THE END

"Mort, I'll sneak behind the Gorillas. Then you distract them, and get them out of the habitat. Got it?" you ask.

"Anything for King Julien!" Mort says.

You carefully climb into the gorilla habitat. You tiptoe around the Gorillas. You are inches away from the bananas when you hear Mort. He's jumping up and down and yelling.

"Hey, giant monkeys! There is no penguin trying to steal your bananas, so don't look behind you!"

With a sinking feeling, you realize that Mort isn't the brightest banana in the bunch. The two hulking gorillas wake up and turn around. You freeze.

"Look what we got here, Bing," says Bada.

"A banana thief."

"No, it's not," says Bing. "It's a back scratcher."

The gorilla picks you up by the feet and uses you like a back scratcher. You have a feeling that he's not going to let you go soon. That means no bananas—and probably no Bananapalooza!

THE END